Meanwhile, the country mouse was hard at work preparing for the town mouse's visit.

After a long journey, the town mouse arrived. The cousins greeted each other joyfully.

"Hello!"

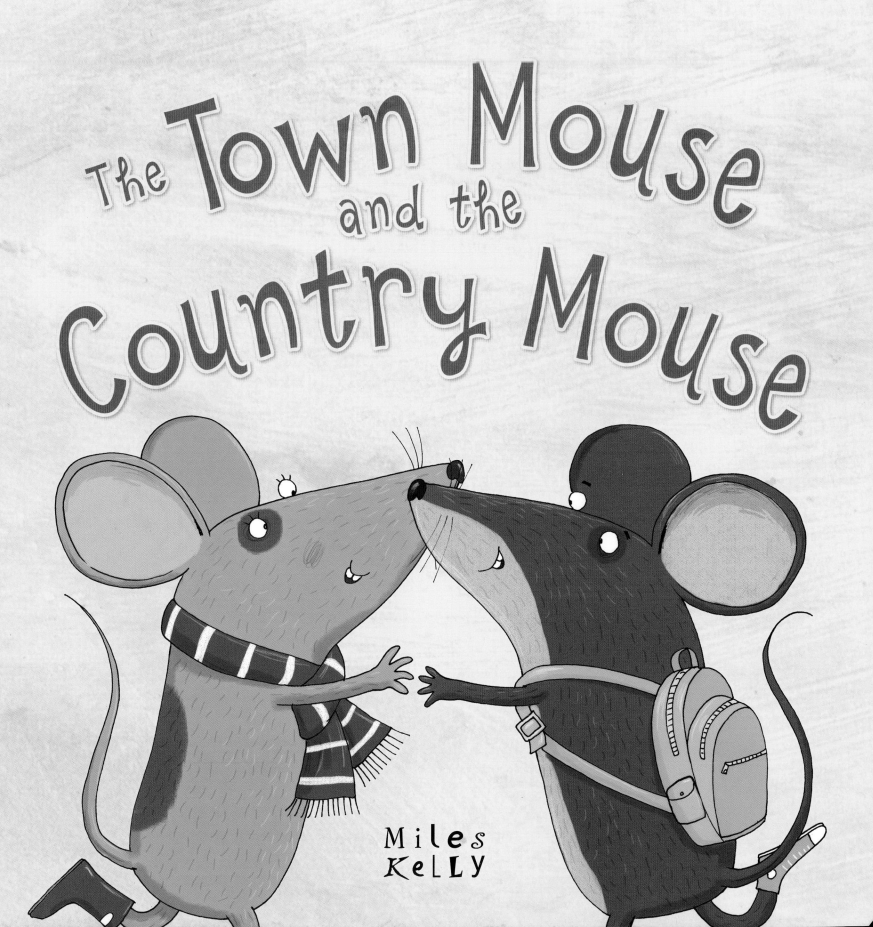

The Town Mouse and the Country Mouse

Miles Kelly

A little mouse who lived in a busy, bustling town was on a train to the country. He was going to visit his cousin. The town mouse was excited, as he had never been to the country before.

The country mouse showed off her home in a tree trunk. It was simple, but warm and cosy. "It doesn't look much like my home," the town mouse said.

Once the town mouse had rested, the country mouse took him to meet the farm animals next door. They crowded round to greet him.

Curious, the horse lowered his head and sniffed at the town mouse. "Watch it!" he cried. He wasn't keen on these new animals.

That evening, the country mouse
served a dinner of bread and cheese.
It was not at all like the fancy meals
the town mouse was used to.

All night, the town mouse tossed
and turned in his bed of leaves.

He was used to sleeping in
a much softer bed.

"How do you put up with this?" the town mouse asked in the morning. "Your food is plain and you sleep on leaves!"

"Come to the town with me and I'll show you how to live."

The country mouse was eager to see the town, so she agreed.

The town mouse lived in a grand house in the middle of town. The country mouse was amazed.

Inside, the town mouse proudly showed off his home. It was very **comfortable**.

The town mouse began a tour of the house. In the kitchen, they spotted a cat prowling around.

"Hide!" the town mouse whispered.

"Shhhhh!"

They scurried under a cup. Here they waited, hardly daring to breathe.

At last, the cat stalked away. "That was close!" exclaimed the country mouse, trembling.

Next, they crept into the living room. There were people there, watching a bright, glowing screen. The country mouse gazed at it –

she had never seen anything like it!

In the playroom, there were all kinds of toys. The country mouse knocked over a tower of building blocks, which came tumbling down.

Crash!

They then went to the dining room.
On the table, they found a

delicious-looking feast.

There were sandwiches and pies, cakes and biscuits – everything that was good to eat. The mice helped themselves.

"I've never had food like this before!" mumbled the country mouse. The town mouse laughed. "This is how you could eat all the time!" he replied.

"Yummy!"

Suddenly, the mice heard growling and scratching at the door.

Two dogs burst in, sniffing the air.

The dogs began to bark, jumping up at the table.

The mice scampered away in fear.

Enough was enough.
The country mouse said goodbye
and left the town at once.

"Goodbye!"

"Better to live
poorly in peace
than richly in fear,"
she said.